FIZZY'S LUNCH LAB

First edition 2014

Library of Congress Catalog Card Number 2013944010
ISBN 978-0-7636-7279-9 (hardcover)
ISBN 978-0-7636-6883-9 (paperback)

14 15 16 17 18 19 TLF 10 9 8 7 6 5 4 3 2 1
Printed in Dongguan, Guangdong, China

This book was typeset in Frutiger and Cafeteria.
The illustrations were created digitally.

Candlewick Entertainment
An imprint of Candlewick Press
99 Dover Street
Somerville, Massachusetts 02144

visit us at www.candlewick.com

SUPER SUPPER
THROWDOWN

CANDLEWICK
ENTERTAINMENT

FREEZER BURN
Rock 'n' Roll Reinforcements

CORPORAL CUP
Recipe Toughie

SULLY THE CELL
Our Guide to the Human Body

TOGETHER, THEY FIGHT THE GREASE-MONGER FAST FOOD FREDDY
Oily Owner of the Fast-Food Theme Park, Greasy World

THE SUPER SUPPER THROWDOWN

Greetings, and welcome to the Lunch Lab!

I'm Professor Fizzy, inventor of this fantabulous high-tech kitchen and its amazing array of handy gadgets. This is where I cook up food and FUN. With my helping hands, of course. . . .

Meet the Lunch Labbers—best friends Avril and Henry, along with my do-it-all invention, Mixie Bot! Henry and Avril are great at taste-testing, and even better at reminding me when I forget stuff. Mixie Bot makes sure the kitchen is running smoothly and is our guide to appliances and safety.

Together, we work to fight the grease-monger Fast Food Freddy. He's the oily owner of the fast-food theme park, Greasy World.

Hello, Fizzy. I'm here to challenge *you* to a cook-off! I call it . . . the Super Supper Throwdown! Each of us will make a dinner, and then some kid guests will judge their favorite at five thirty this evening. If you win, I'll serve your meal at Greasy World for a month. If I win, you have to eat my greasy grub. What do you say, Fizzy? Are you in? Or are you *out*?

Hmm. Replace a greasy meal with a fresh one of mine? I'm *in*. Challenge accepted! But, great gazpacho! I have less than two hours. We better get started, gang.

My Friend Food Plate

To defeat Freddy, we'll need to create a balanced meal that's not only tasty but also good for you. Planning a balanced, tasty, healthful meal is a snap once you know my good buddy Food Plate.

Check me out! I have space for each of the food groups: fruits, vegetables, grains, and protein, plus a glass for dairy products like milk.

To know how much food to serve, use Food Plate's easy-to-follow method:

- Fill half your plate with fruits and vegetables.
- Fill one quarter of your plate with whole grains.
- Fill one quarter of your plate with protein.

Easy, right? Now we can create a meal that's full of fresh ingredients.

Hmm. I wonder what Freddy is planning.

Meanwhile, at Greasy World...

Heh, heh. I'm planning a meal based on Fast Food Freddy's Junk-Food Plate:

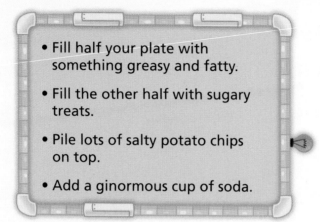

- Fill half your plate with something greasy and fatty.

- Fill the other half with sugary treats.

- Pile lots of salty potato chips on top.

- Add a ginormous cup of soda.

Voilà! Instant Super Supper Throwdown winner.

And I have something the judges won't be able to resist—a doll that looks just like ME! Kids don't care about the food. They just want a free toy.

Fizzy doesn't stand a chance. I'm going to win!

SHOP THE U

OK, Lunch Labbers, let's pop open the pantry and see what ingredients we have. . . . Good gravy! It's empty!

Nothing in the fridge, either. And the only thing in the freezer is our house band.

"How's it going, Freezer Burn?"

It's lonely in here, Fizzy.

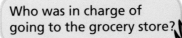

Who was in charge of going to the grocery store?

You were, Professor. See?

Oh, er, ha. Not a problem. We'll just take the gang on a mission. To the grocery store!

Don't despair. The grocery store might look confusing, but I have a trick for finding good food. It's called shopping the U!

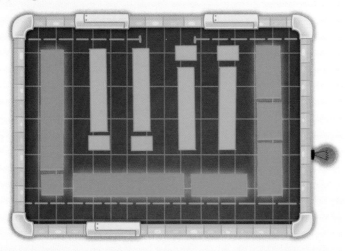

Imagine you're looking at the grocery store from above. Each type of food has its own section. The best foods for you—the ones with fewest preservatives and chemicals—are on the outside edges of the store. There you'll find produce, meat, bread, and dairy.

The middle tends to have processed and frozen foods, all that Fast Food Freddy stuff.

Freddy's Freezer Shopping

Psst, kids! Don't listen to Fizzy. You can get everything you need here in the freezer section. Then just zap it in the microwave. Like my new stick-o-fish here. It's fish—on a stick!

Whoa. This ingredients list is HUGE. Look at all those preservatives.

No, thanks, Freddy. We like fresh foods better. Professor Fizzy taught us well—shop the U and always check labels.

Be a Label Detective

To find out if a food is healthful, sleuth out its ingredients list for clues.

Clue #1:
The ingredients used *most* are listed first. Beware of an ingredients list that starts with sugars, fats, oils, or salt.

Clue #2:
Shorter is better. Often, the longer the list, the less natural and healthful the food is.

Clue #3:
Look for natural ingredients you recognize. Skip foods with lots of chemical names that are difficult to say.

Come on, kiddos. Let's hurry back to the lab and whip up a winner!

Now that our fridge and pantry are stocked, let's get cooking! You folks at home can cook with your family. Pitch in by measuring ingredients, rinsing produce, or assembling the foods you'll need.

Nothing has to be perfect— enjoy yourself and be creative. Just remember to follow my kitchen safety tips.

Fizzy's Kitchen Safety Tips

1. *Always cook with a grown-up!* Never use a knife, the oven, or the microwave without an adult.

2. Wash your hands before cooking and after handling raw food.

3. To avoid cross-contamination, don't use a cutting board that was used for raw food. Wash it first.

4. Turn pot handles inward so that you won't bump into one and knock the pot over.

5. Stay away from electric sockets, especially if your hands are wet. And keep electric appliances away from water to avoid shocks.

EAT A RAINBOW

When creating a meal, make a rainbow. A food rainbow, that is. Foods that are the same color tend to have the same vitamins and minerals. So if you want to eat well, eat a bunch of different colors.

Red produce, like strawberries and radishes, have antioxidants that keep cells healthy.

Orange and yellow foods, like carrots and corn, have carotenoids for healthy eyes.

From blue blueberries to green broccoli, if you eat a rainbow of colors, you're sure to get all the vitamins your body needs.

Fast Food Freddy steers clear of fruit and veggies, so most of his food comes in two colors: brown and gray. Ick! We can beat him with a colorful dish, such as Green Salad with Lime Dressing.

"Corporal Cup, can you give us the recipe?"

Food Fact

Try to eat two cups of fruit and two cups of veggies every day.

You got it, Fizzy. Attention, cooking cadets! My job is to make sure that all Professor Fizzy's recipes go according to plan. I'm one tough cup, but I think you kids will measure up.

Green Salad with Lime Dressing

VEGETARIAN	TIME	DIFFICULTY	SERVES
V	🕐	**M**	**4**
YES	Under 30 minutes	Medium	

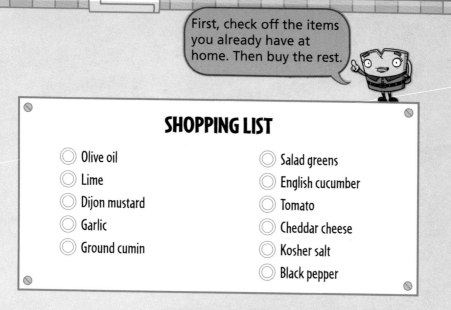

First, check off the items you already have at home. Then buy the rest.

SHOPPING LIST

- ◯ Olive oil
- ◯ Lime
- ◯ Dijon mustard
- ◯ Garlic
- ◯ Ground cumin

- ◯ Salad greens
- ◯ English cucumber
- ◯ Tomato
- ◯ Cheddar cheese
- ◯ Kosher salt
- ◯ Black pepper

YOU WILL NEED

For the dressing:

3 to 4 tablespoons olive oil

2 tablespoons fresh lime juice

1 teaspoon Dijon mustard

1 garlic clove, minced

1/4 teaspoon ground cumin

kosher salt and pepper to taste

For the salad:

8 cups salad greens

1/2 English cucumber, sliced

1 large tomato, diced

1/4 cup diced cheddar cheese

DIRECTIONS

**Add any other colorful fruit or veggie you wish.
Smoked Gouda makes a flavorful substitution for the cheddar.**

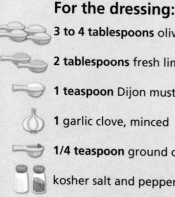

STEP 1: To make the dressing, place all the ingredients in a small bowl and whisk well.

STEP 2: To make the salad, place all the ingredients in a large bowl and drizzle with the dressing.

STEP 3: Mix well and serve immediately.

Fizzy's Goggle Inspection

"Thanks, Corporal Cup!"

Now let's check in with Freddy to see what he's making.

Nom, nom . . . er, hi Fizzy. Just trying my side dish, Sugar-Bomb Jelly Beans. Since they're different colors, they must be good for me.

Not so fast. Only *natural* colors from real fruits and vegetables count. Freddy's jelly beans are full of artificial colors.

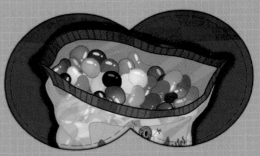

Now take a look at a salad using the Lunch Lab goggles. It's full of vitamins.

Food Fact

Vitamin A in carrots can help you see in the dark because it prevents night blindness.

PROTEIN POWER!

We'll need a protein dish to go with that salad. The best sources of protein are lean meats, milk, beans, nuts, and eggs. (No yolking!)

What's protein? It's simple. Proteins are the building blocks of muscle and bone, the parts of our body that make us strong. Your skin, hair, and fingernails are also mostly made of protein.

But don't take my word for it. Let my old pal Sully the Cell show you. He'll be your personal guide through the busy highways inside the human body. Hop in his cab for an up-close-and-personal tour!

"Sully, can you show our newest Lunch Labber how our muscles use protein?"

Food Fact

Each pound of muscle in your body burns 75–100 calories every day, and that's before exercise!

Sure. Nice to meet you, kid.

Muscle Beach

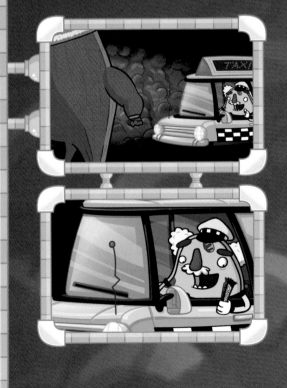

"Ah, there's Marty the Muscle Cell!"

"Hey, Sully."

"What's it like when the body eats a candy bar? It's got lots of sugar and fat, but very little protein."

"Eh, I can't do much with it."

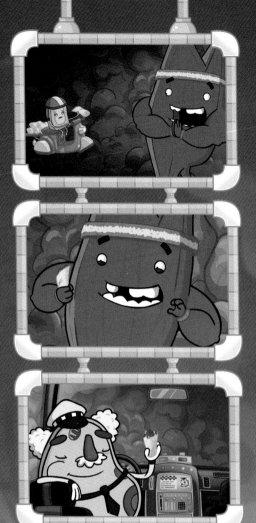

"Delivery for Marty! Professor Fizzy's Black-Bean Burritos!"

"Now, this makes me feel fantastic! Pull-up contest, Sully?"

"Well, there you have it, kids. Muscles love protein. And so do cells that haven't had lunch yet. Mmm."

Those burritos remind me of another one of my protein-packed creations—the Veggilicious Hoagie. It will be just the ticket to win this throwdown. Can you help us out, Corporal Cup?

SHOPPING LIST

- Whole-wheat sandwich rolls
- Provolone cheese
- Roasted or smoked turkey
- Lettuce
- Tomato
- Green or red bell pepper
- Cucumber
- Red onion

YOU WILL NEED

4 whole-wheat sandwich rolls

1/2 cup homemade Groovy Guacamole (see recipe on page 26)

3 ounces sliced cheese

4 ounces turkey

1 1/2 cups shredded lettuce

1 large tomato, thinly sliced

1 green or red bell pepper, sliced into strips

1 medium cucumber, thinly sliced

1/2 small red onion, thinly sliced

DIRECTIONS

STEP 1: Open up the sandwich rolls and spread some Groovy Guacamole on the top halves.

STEP 2: Place some cheese and turkey on the bottom halves.

STEP 3: Top each with some lettuce, tomato, bell pepper, cucumber, and red onion.

STEP 4: Put the sandwiches together and serve!

Fizzy's Pick-Me-Ups	Freddy's Energy Zappers

veggies with hummus

sticky buns

tuna sandwich

deep-fried chicken wings

homemade energy bar

candy bar

FATS: THE GOOD, THE BAD, AND THE NASTY

And now for a word about my favorite ingredient!
Our Veggilicious Hoagies really sing with a spread of Groovy Guacamole.

Ha! Your guacamole and avocados have fat, too. Just like my throwdown-winning doughnuts.

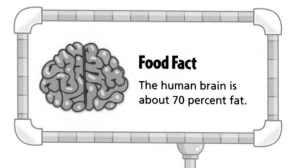

Food Fact

The human brain is about 70 percent fat.

Fizzy's Goggle Inspection

Freddy is right. But avocados and guacamole have the good kind of fat—unsaturated fat.

It's very different from the trans fat found in processed junk foods.

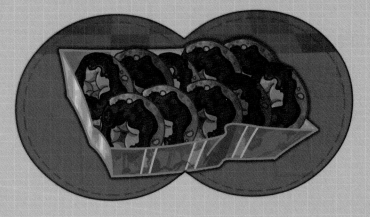

Good fat is important for your skin and organs, and it gives you warmth and energy. The bad fats, on the other hand, can lead to clogged arteries, heart problems, and obesity.

How can you tell the difference between good fat and bad fat? Well, if it comes straight from the plant to your plate, it's probably got good fat. There are three main types of fat—the good, the bad, and the nasty.

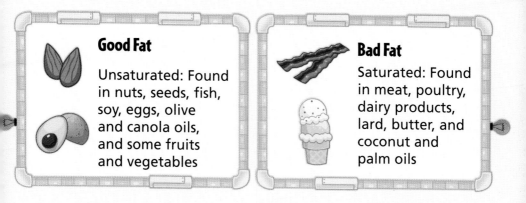

Good Fat

Unsaturated: Found in nuts, seeds, fish, soy, eggs, olive and canola oils, and some fruits and vegetables

Bad Fat

Saturated: Found in meat, poultry, dairy products, lard, butter, and coconut and palm oils

Nasty Fat

Trans fat: Found in deep-fried foods, crackers, cookies, cake, shortening, and margarine. Trans fat is a human-made fat that is added to processed foods to make them last longer. To find it, look for partially hydrogenated oils in the ingredients list.

That's nasty stuff! Unlike our Groovy Guacamole. "Could you give us a hand with it, Corporal Cup?"

OK, cadets! Get ready to squish, squash, and smash some avocados. That's an order.

Groovy Guacamole

VEGETARIAN	TIME	DIFFICULTY	SERVES
V	🕐	**M**	**4**
YES	Under 30 minutes	Medium	

SHOPPING LIST

- ⬡ Avocados
- ⬡ Tomato
- ⬡ Cilantro
- ⬡ Red onion
- ⬡ Lime
- ⬡ Cayenne pepper
- ⬡ Kosher salt

YOU WILL NEED

 2 ripe avocados, peeled, pitted, and chopped

 1/2 cup chopped fresh tomato

1/4 cup chopped fresh cilantro

2 tablespoons chopped red onion

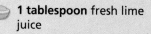 **1 tablespoon** fresh lime juice

A pinch of cayenne pepper

 A pinch of kosher salt

DIRECTIONS

STEP 1: Using a fork, coarsely mash the avocado in a medium bowl. Then add the other ingredients and mix.

STEP 2: Cover and chill the guacamole for half an hour to blend the flavors. Serve.

Fizzy's Good Fats	Freddy's Bad Fats

**whole-wheat quesadilla
with low-fat cheese**

**fried frozen fish
(on a stick!)**

**sliced bananas with
peanut butter**

**packaged
doughnuts**

**whole-wheat English
muffin veggie pizza**

frozen pepperoni pizza

To make true heroes of our hoagies, use whole-wheat rolls. Remember: If the flour is wheat, *sweet*! If the flour is white, eh, it's all right.

That's because white flour is processed, so most of the good stuff like fiber, vitamins, and minerals is sucked out. With wheat flour, all the good stuff is left in.

ZAP!

What on earth is—?

Behold! My latest greasy creation, the Pizzanator! I smell a Super Supper Throwdown winner.

Food Fact

The longest loaf of bread in the United States measured 2,357 feet!

Fizzy's Goggle Inspection

The only thing I smell is trouble. The Pizzanator's processed flour levels are off the charts! Freddy had better try again—with wheat crust.

Wheat has complex carbohydrates, which give you lots of energy.

Think of carbs as gasoline for your body. You need them to run your body's engine. When your parents buy gas for their car, they choose the kind that will make it run best. There are different types of gas for cars, and there are different types of carbs in foods.

COMPLEX carbs give you long-lasting energy and are often rich in vitamins, minerals, and fiber. Your body uses them slowly so you can play baseball or ride a bike.

SIMPLE carbs give you quick energy. Your body burns through them quickly. Before you know it, you're hungry again. Plus, simple carbs don't offer much when it comes to vitamins, minerals, or fiber.

Fizzy's Complex Carbs	Freddy's Simple Carbs

packaged cookies

whole-wheat bread

apple

candy apple (on a stick!)

veggie burger
on a whole-wheat bun

bacon double
cheeseburger

Hmm. Now, what goes well with hoagies?

I've got it! No, wait—I lost it. What were we talking about again? Oh, right. Something munchy and *crunchy,* like my fiber-packed tortilla chips. Fiber is the body's plumber—er, not quite like Carla, the plumber here. . . . Fiber keeps your body's pipes unclogged and eliminates toxins.

Fiber can be found in lots of fruits, vegetables, nuts, and beans. Eating Freddy's fatty foods, however, can block those pipes and lead to digestion congestion.

So remember to decrease the grease. Tell us more, Sully!

You bet. Buckle up because we're headed for the small intestine.

Fiber Cowboys

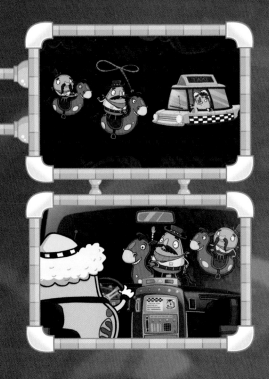

"Yee-haw! Get along, you little undigested varmints! No lollygagging!"

"Howdy, fellas."

"Howdy yourself, city slicker."

"Can you fiber cowboys explain what you do?"

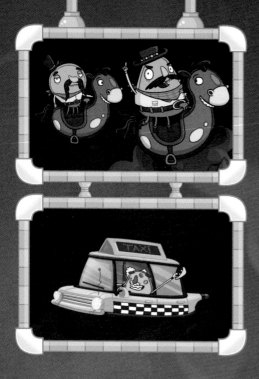

"We're the law 'round these parts. We keep everything moving, so there's less time for anything unhealthy to get absorbed into the body."

"Thanks, fellas! Giddyup, you big yellow cab."

Yee-haw! To help the fiber cowboys keep your body healthy, eat five servings of fiber every day. Avril and Henry, can you think of five sources of fiber?

What about an orange? And a salad with dinner?

Cereal with bananas! An apple! Oh, and veggie bean chili!

"Hey, Corporal Cup! We're ready to make those fiberiffic tortilla chips now."

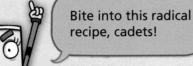

Bite into this radical recipe, cadets!

Tortilla Chips

VEGETARIAN	TIME	DIFFICULTY	SERVES
V	**L**	**M**	**4**
YES	Under 30 minutes	Medium	

SHOPPING LIST

◎ Whole-wheat flour tortillas
◎ Canola or vegetable oil
◎ Kosher salt

YOU WILL NEED

4 eight-inch whole-wheat flour tortillas

1 tablespoon canola or vegetable oil

1/4 teaspoon kosher salt

DIRECTIONS

Corn tortillas may be substituted for the wheat tortillas.

STEP 1: Adjust the oven rack to the middle position, and preheat the oven to 425 degrees.

STEP 2: Using your hands, rub each tortilla with oil, then sprinkle it with salt.

STEP 3: Cut each tortilla into 8 triangles (the way you'd slice a pizza), and place them on a baking sheet. Bake until lightly golden, about 5 minutes.

STEP 4: Set aside to cool. Serve.

Bah! Who cares about fiber? I'll be serving my double-fried potato chips. They taste great with my double-fried chicken nuggets, double-fried onion rings, double-fried cheesecake . . . Oof! Why isn't my stomach happy with me?

CALCIUM-YUM-YUM

Double-fried cheesecake? Double blech! We can come up with a tastier dessert that will make your body happy.

I know what you're thinking . . . can dessert be healthy? Of course! Especially if it's Berry Banana Fro-Yo. We're talking vitamin-packed fruit and calcium-rich yogurt.

Calcium is good for strong teeth and bones. You'll find it in dairy products like milk, ice cream, and cheese, as well as in oranges, broccoli, and salmon. Shoot for three cups of low-fat dairy products a day. Your bones will thank you.

Speaking of bones, Sully has a friend he'd like you to meet. . . .

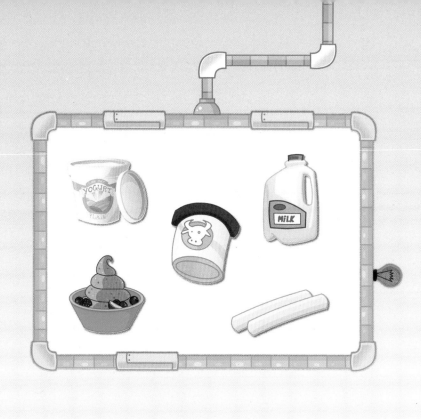

Meet Bobby, the humerus bone. He's a real wisecracker.

Bobby, the Humerus Bone

"Sully! Do I have a bone to pick with you."

"Ha, ha! I brought you your favorite— calcium."

"Milk, cheese, yogurt . . . It's so easy to get one hundred percent of the recommended daily serving, even a lazybones can do it."

"Calcium keeps me strong. Because bones don't like to take a . . . *break*. Get it?"

"Good one, Bobby. They don't call you a funny bone for nothing!"

Thanks for helping us bone up on our calcium facts, Sully! Over to you, Corporal Cup.

This fro-yo dessert is a cool idea. Get mixing, cadet!

Berry Banana Fro-Yo

VEGETARIAN	TIME	DIFFICULTY	SERVES
V	🕐	**M**	**4**
YES	Under 30 minutes	Medium	

SHOPPING LIST

⊘ Frozen berries
⊘ Bananas
⊘ Low-fat yogurt

YOU WILL NEED

2 cups frozen berries

2 overripe bananas, peeled, sliced thin, and frozen

1 cup plain low-fat yogurt

DIRECTIONS

STEP 1: Place the frozen fruit in a food processor or blender and blend until smooth.

STEP 2: Add the yogurt and blend until completely mixed. Serve immediately.

Attention, Lunch Labbers! It is I, Fast Food Freddy. Check out my newest creation, Frozen Cheese Chunks! They've got lots of calcium. Uh, that's good for you, right?

Gross. There are tastier ways to get calcium.

Freddy, why don't you try Fizzy's fro-yo instead?

Fizzy's Calci-yum Treats	Freddy's Calci-yuck Eats

string cheese

**frozen cheese chunks
(on a stick!)**

strawberry smoothie

milk shake

**veggies with
cottage-cheese dip**

**nachos with
processed-cheese dip**

HYDRATION NATION

Our Super Supper is nearly done. All we have left to do is choose a drink.

We already know that Freddy will serve a super-size soda with his dinner. That's the worst of the worst. Sugary soda gives you quick energy, but then you crash. Plus, it adds inches to your waistline.

We'll stick with water. Since water makes up about sixty percent of your body, it'll always float your boat. If you don't drink enough, you might feel tired or cranky. You might even imagine that you're hungry, when you're actually thirsty.

The best ways to hydrate are to drink water, milk, and fruit juice, and to eat watery foods like fruits, vegetables, and soup.

Food Fact

In one hour of exercise, the body can lose more than a quart of water.

Yummo! Our Super Supper looks deeeeeelicious! Just in time, too. It's almost five thirty. Let's see if Freddy is ready. . . . Oh, dear. Freddy doesn't look so good.

Ooooh! I ate on the run, and now I don't feel so good. I'll, er, just share my dinnertime advice from the ground. Ugh.

Freddy's Gobble-on-the-Go Tips

- Dinner tables take up too much space. Fast food is where it's at. So come on down to Greasy World and gobble on the go!

- Eating is like a race—do it fast. Don't bother to chew. But if you must, at least do it with your mouth open.

- See how many things you can do while scarfing down your dinner. Can you watch TV, talk on the phone, and play video games at the same time? If so, you're a dinner winner!

"Game over, Freddy."

No wonder he doesn't feel well. I get a tummy ache just hearing those tips. Doesn't Freddy know that dinner should be enjoyed? That means sitting at the table with family to relax, laugh, and catch up on everyone's day.

Families who eat together communicate better and build stronger relationships. Plus, kids who eat family meals get more calcium, iron, fiber, and vitamins than those who don't. Family meals can even help you do better in school!

Avril's family used to be too busy to eat together. It made her sad. But then she came up with a great idea—this family dinner checklist.

Avril's Checklist for Family Dinner Fun

1. Turn off the TV.

2. Put away all screens—video games, phones, etc. You can get them back after dinner.

3. *Cook* a meal. Don't zap one in the microwave.

4. Everything's easier when you work together. Each person should pick one job they like to do, such as setting the table or filling the water glasses.

5. Eat together at the table, and talk for at least thirty minutes. Give it a try—you might like it!

6. Take turns saying tongue twisters. Can you say this three times fast? "The family table beats microwave dinners and cable."

Henry's Conversation Starters

Get the conversation going at your family table with these questions:

• If you could have any superpower, what would it be?

• If you could be any famous person for a day, who would you choose?

• If you could go anywhere in the world, where would you go?

• What's your favorite animal?

• What was the best part of your day?

How to Set the Table

Hi! We're the Lunch Lab's handy-dandy utensils, here to show you a trick for remembering how to set the table.

Picture the word *FORKS*. The order of a place setting, from left to right, is: *F* for the fork, *O* for the plate (because of its shape), *K* for the knife, and *S* for the spoon. Place knives with their cutting edge toward the plate. The napkin goes under the fork or on the plate.

Food Fact

Eating family meals together helps kids learn routines and family traditions.

Fizzy's Super Supper

Green Salad with Lime Dressing
Veggilicious Hoagie with Groovy Guacamole
Tortilla Chips
Berry Banana Fro-Yo
Water or Milk

Time's up. Utensils down. It's throwdown time.

Woo-hoo! We did it, gang. We planned a perfectly balanced meal. It has veggies, fruits, protein, good fat, complex carbohydrates, fiber, and calcium. Best of all, it's knock-your-socks-off scrumptious! Freddy's menu, on the other hand, is full of fat, sugar, and salt. Who do you think will win?

Freddy's Not-So-Super Supper

Sugar-Bomb Jelly Beans

Bacon Double Cheeseburger

Double-Fried Potato Chips

Frozen Cheese Chunks (on a stick!)

Soda

A FREE TOY!

The kid taste-testers are already blindfolded and sitting at the judges' table. They can't see what's on the dishes in front of them.

Dish number one is Freddy's Bacon Double Cheeseburger, dripping with grease. Eww.

Dish number two is our Veggilicious Hoagie.

Just out of curiosity, let's take a look at that food.

Fizzy's Goggle Inspection

Whoa! Freddy's cheeseburger is loaded with calories.

Calories are the amount of energy inside our food. Our bodies need a certain number of calories each day. But Freddy's meal has way too many. You'd need to spend all day exercising to burn them off.

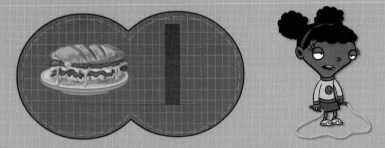

Our Veggilicious Hoagie, on the other hand, has fewer calories. You'd only have to do some light exercising to burn those off.

Yeah, but where's the TOY? No kid will be able to pass up my Freddy doll. Ha, ha! I'm going to win.

I hope he's wrong. The judges are each taking a bite. Oooh, I'm nervous.

Leaping lima beans! We won, Lunch Labbers! We're the Super Supper Throwdown champions!

I hope Freddy has learned a lesson. Kids care about more than toys. They also care about tasty meals they can enjoy with those they love. Because families who eat together are the real winners.

Well, I better banana split. I'm off to make a *lot* more hoagies for Freddy to sell all this month at Greasy World.

Good work, Lunch Labber! See you next time.